Amos's Sweater

BY

Janet Lunn

PICTURES BY

Kim LaFave

Groundwood Books
House of Anansi Press
Toronto Berkeley

AMOS was old and Amos was cold
and Amos was tired of giving away all his wool.

So one summer day when Aunt Hattie went out to the pasture with her big clipping shears, Amos balked.

"Baa," he cried. He butted Aunt Hattie. And ran away.

"Amos, stop!" shouted Aunt Hattie. "Stop, Amos!" But Amos did not stop.

Aunt Hattie ran after him. She chased him around and around the meadow. She chased him up and down the hillside and across the brook. But Amos was too fast. Uncle Henry had to help catch him and hold him down. Then Aunt Hattie clipped his wool.

“There, now, Amos,” she said. “That wasn’t so bad, was it?”

“Baa,” said Amos.

Aunt Hattie gave him an apple to make him feel better. But Amos did not feel better. He was old and he was cold and now he was angry.

Aunt Hattie washed the wool. She combed it and she spun it. Then she knitted it into a big, warm sweater for Uncle Henry.

"Isn't that fine, Amos?" She showed him the big, warm sweater.

"Baa." Amos snatched at the sweater with his teeth.

Every time Amos saw Uncle Henry wearing his sweater he bit it. There were always Amos holes in it that Aunt Hattie had to mend.

One hot day, when Uncle Henry left the sweater over the fence, Amos tried to pull it down. It stuck fast and he made such a huge hole in it Aunt Hattie came after him with a stick.

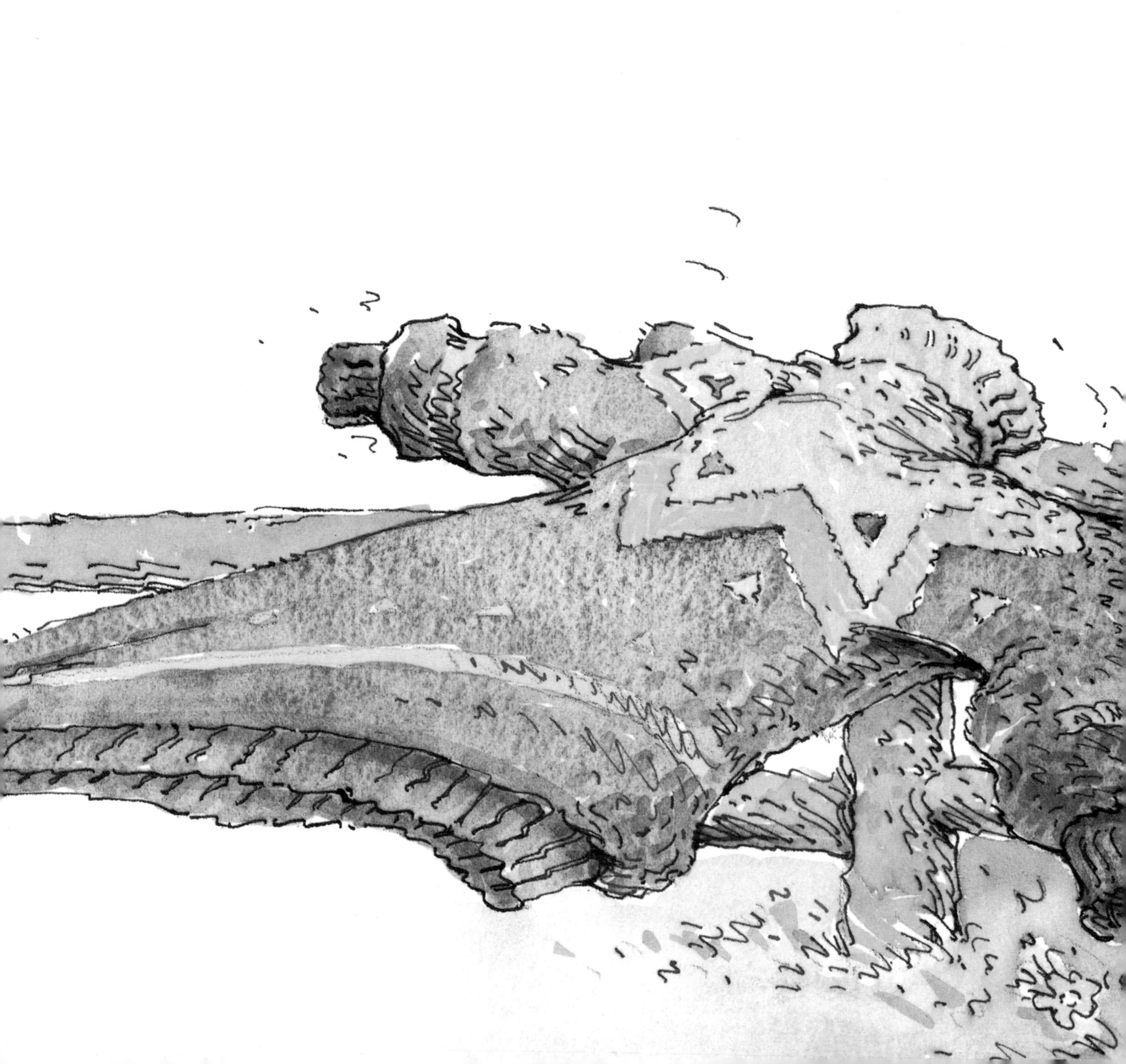

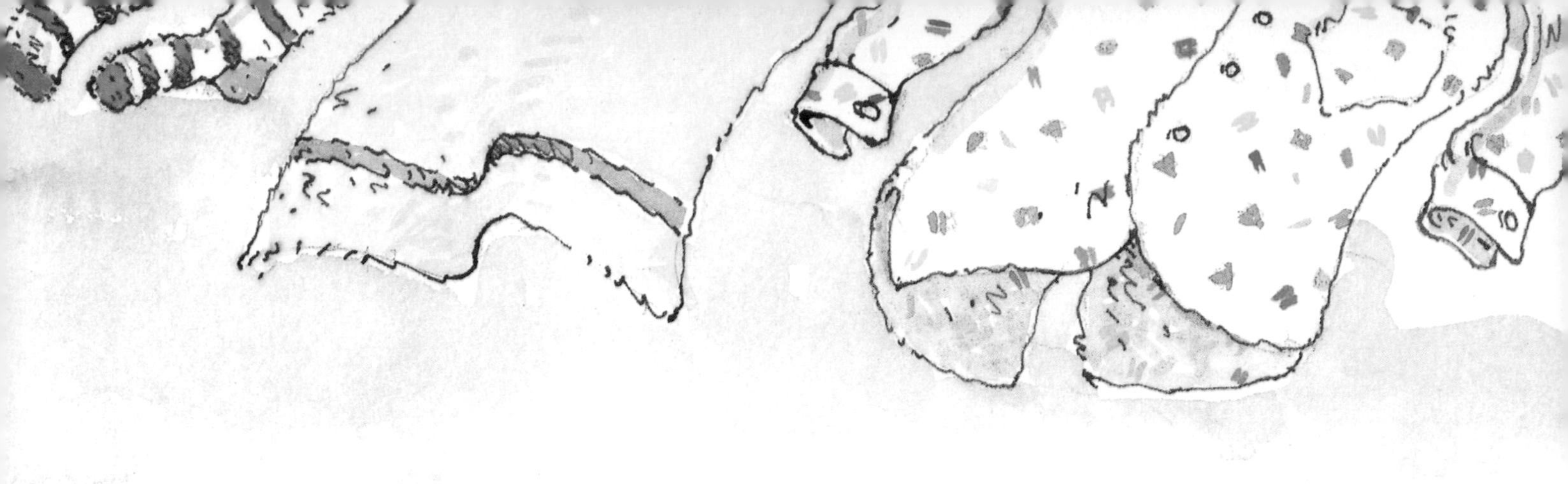

Aunt Hattie mended the huge hole. She washed the sweater and hung it out to dry. Amos waited for her to go back into the house.

Then he made a jump for it. But the line was too high.

One night, Uncle Henry left the sweater on the table in the back kitchen of the house. The door was open. The moon was full. Amos could see the sweater from his stall in the barn.

He butted the stall door. He shoved it. He butted it, he shoved it. He butted and shoved until the door flew open.

He dashed across the barnyard into the back kitchen. He yanked the sweater off the table. Furiously he pulled it this way and that. An end of yarn caught in his hoof.

He pulled and twisted to get it loose. He tugged. He twisted. He bit. He rolled around on the floor. The more he struggled the tighter the yarn wound around him. Soon he was so tangled you couldn't tell which was yarn, which was sweater, which was Amos.

“Baa,” he cried, “Baa, baaaaa,” in such rage Aunt Hattie and Uncle Henry came running to see what had happened.

“Oh, Amos. Now you’ve done it!” Aunt Hattie sighed. Uncle Henry laughed. He began to unwind the yarn. Amos glared at them with his angry black eyes.

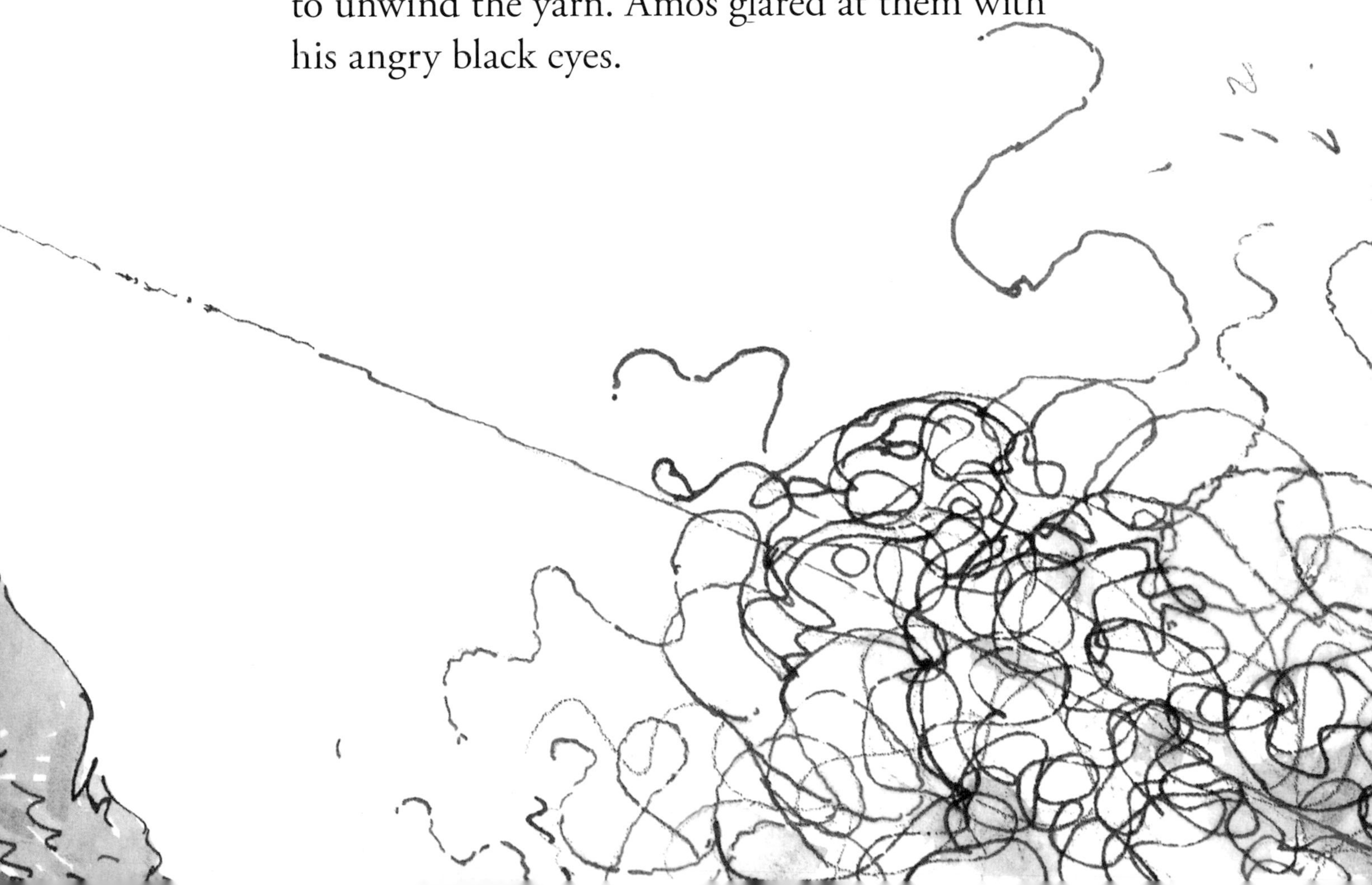

Free at last, he stood up. His two front legs were deep in the arms of Uncle Henry's sweater. His head poked through the top.

"You know, Hattie, Amos is old," said Uncle Henry.

"And maybe Amos is cold," said Aunt Hattie.

"And maybe," they said, both at the same time, "Amos is tired of giving away all his wool."

Now, if you go by the farm where Aunt Hattie and Uncle Henry live, you will see the sheep out in the pasture. There is one, standing a little apart. That is Amos.

He is old. But he is not cold because he is wearing his sweater.

For Peg, for Amos and for Ted,
with love

J.L.

For Carol and Jeffrey and baby

K.L.

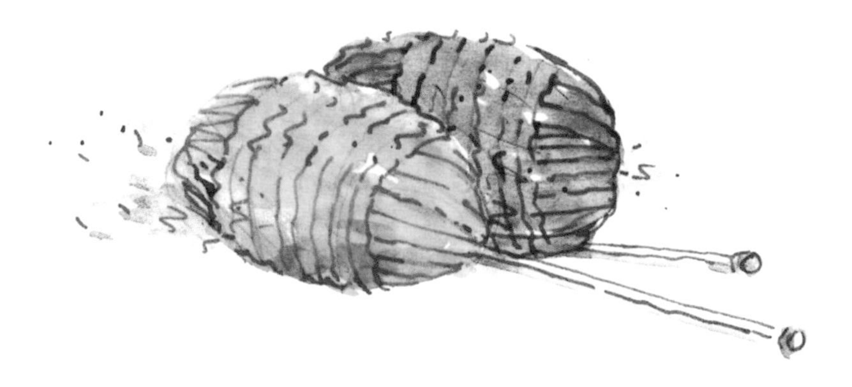

First Meadow Mouse paperback edition 1994
New paperback edition 2007
Fourth printing 2015

Groundwood Books / House of Anansi Press
110 Spadina Avenue, Suite 801, Toronto, Ontario M5V 2K4
or c/o Publishers Group West
1700 Fourth Street, Berkeley, CA 94710

We acknowledge for their financial support of our publishing program the Canada Council for the Arts, the Government of Canada and the Ontario Arts Council.

Canada Council for the Arts
Conseil des Arts du Canada

With the participation of the Government of Canada
Avec la participation du gouvernement du Canada

Library and Archives Canada Cataloguing in Publication
Lunn, Janet
Amos's sweater / by Janet Lunn ; pictures by Kim LaFave.
ISBN 978-0-88899-845-3
1. Sheep–Juvenile fiction. I. LaFave, Kim II. Title.
PS8573.U55A8 2007 jC813'.54 C2007-901148-9

Printed and bound in Malaysia